In loving memory of Philip Duncan Harnick:
Creative, talented, generous, remarkable. —R.T.

Copyright © 2016 by Richard Torrey

All rights reserved. Published in the United States by Doubleday,
an imprint of Random House Children's Books,
a division of Penguin Random House LLC, New York.

Doubleday and the colophon are registered trademarks of Penguin Random House LLC.

Visit us on the Web! randomhousekids.com

Educators and librarians, for a variety of teaching tools, visit us at RHTeachersLibrarians.com

Library of Congress Cataloging-in-Publication Data
Torrey, Rich, author, illustrator.
The almost terrible playdate / by Richard Torrey. — First edition.
pages cm
Summary: "A young boy and girl, with very different ideas about what they want to play,
face off during a playdate." —Provided by publisher.
ISBN 978-0-553-51099-7 (trade) — ISBN 978-0-375-97430-4 (lib. bdg.) — ISBN 978-0-553-51100-0 (ebook)
[1. Play—Fiction. 2. Imagination—Fiction.] I. Title.
PZ7.T64573Am 2016 [E]—dc23 2015004734

The illustrations for this book were created with PITT oil-based pencils, crayons, and colored pencils.
Book design by Elizabeth Tardiff

MANUFACTURED IN CHINA
10 9 8 7 6 5 4 3 2 1
First Edition

The Almost Terrible Playdate

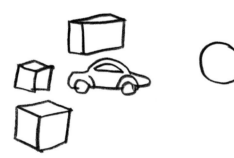

WRITTEN AND ILLUSTRATED BY
Richard Torrey

DOUBLEDAY BOOKS FOR YOUNG READERS

What do you
want to play?

What do *you*
want to play?

How about *I'm* the queen of the universe
and my doll, Pippy, is my sister queen,
and *you* visit my castle?

Or how about *I'm* the giantest dinosaur ever
and *you're* a dinosaur too—but not the giantest—
and we stomp around smashing stuff?

What if *I'm* a magical wizard and Pippy is my helper,
and *you're* a frog that I turn into a pony for Pippy to ride?

Or what if *I'm* a giant fire-breathing dragon
that you find in a cave and I scare you?

No, how about *I'm* a ballet instructor and
you are in my ballet school, and so is Pippy?

RRRRRRRRR!

No, how about we're both race cars but *I'm* the fastest
so I win the Championship of the Universe?

I know! *I'll* be a famous singer in a band with Pippy and *you're* watching our show, and we sing like this: *Oooooooo yeah!*

You sound like a wolf howling. Hey, I know, *you* can be a wolf and *I'll* be a bear and everyone is afraid of us!

No, *you* can be a bear in *my* circus
and Pippy and I train you to do tricks.

I don't want to be in *your* circus.

Well, *I* don't want to be a wolf . . . or a dinosaur . . . or a race car!

And *I* don't want to be a ballerina . . . or a frog . . . or a pony!

I want to be what *I* want to be!

I don't want to play with you!

I'm making a mansion.

I'm making a castle.

I'm a wizard-queen-ballerina-teacher who is also a
famous singer and Pippy is my singing-dancing-sister-queen.
We also own a circus.

And I'm a flying-dragon-race-car, but I can also turn into
a bulldozer, and a dinosaur, and a bear.
And I have my own zoo!

If you're a bulldozer, maybe you can build a road to my castle, and when you get here you can see my singing show.

Okay, and maybe when you're done singing, I can turn into a dragon and give everyone a ride to see my mansion and my zoo!

This is fun!
We should play again tomorrow.

Okay.

What do you
want to play?

What do *you*
want to play?